GOOF TROOP

"THE POWER OF POSITIVE GOOFING"

WELCOME TO SPOONERVILLE, AN AVERAGE TOWN WITH AN AVERAGE POPULATION IN AN AVERAGE PART OF THE COUNTRY!

It has houses, streets, and sidewalks, places for kids to play and adults to relax.

Spoonerville is a nice place to be an adult. It's a great place to be a kid. And it's a quiet, peaceful place to live ... most of the time ...

DAD, LOOK OUT!!

WHOOA!

But Goofy couldn't see where
he was going, so Waffles the cat
got a rude awakening! With a flying leap,
Waffles landed on top of Goofy's head.

Having a frantic cat clinging to his head
didn't help Goofy's balance. Waffles tried
to get away, and Max tried to get out of the
way, but nothing worked. Goofy spun,
tripped, and crashed out the back door,
dragging Max, Waffles, vacuum cleaner,
and cleaning supplies with him.

Of course, Goofy's next-door neighbor Pete was there to see Goofy come to grief.

"Oh. Hi, Pete," Goofy said weakly. "Nice sun-shiny day, isn't it?"

"Yeah," Pete replied with a sneer, "and it'll stay nice through next weekend. We wouldn't want it to rain on the big day, would we?"

"Big day?"

"Sure!" said Pete. "Next Saturday will be Fitness Fun Day. You didn't forget, did you?"

"'Course it is!" Pete said. "And competition means winnin'. And we're gonna win!"

"Right, Dad," said PJ. After Pete and Goofy had gone back inside, PJ squeezed through a loose fence board into Max's yard.

"Dad just wants us to win so we can get our picture in the paper," he complained.

"I don't even want to **go**," Max sighed. "I can see the caption now: 'Klutziest Twosome in Town'!" He hung his head. "But everybody's going to be there. How can I tell Dad that he's part of the reason I don't want to go?"

There was no denying that Goofy was a klutz, and that Max was, too. PJ thought for a bit. What could he do to help his best friend?

"Listen, Max," he began, "my dad always says that when you have a problem, you should face it head-on!"

"Aw, Peej," Max moaned, "your dad's idea of facing a problem head-on is to run it over. How can I face this problem head on? By brain-washing myself?"

PJ didn't answer right away. Of the two friends, Max was usually the upbeat, optimistic one. It took PJ a few minutes to psych himself into the unaccustomed role.

"You're not that far off," he finally suggested. "If you **think** you're a klutz, you'll **be** a klutz. But if you think you're **not** a klutz . . ."

7

The next day, Max and PJ went to the park
to see if all their efforts had paid off.

ALL RIGHT! TIME
TO *CONDITION* MY
SPLIT-SECOND
REFLEXES!

PJ figured that Max was
psyched up enough to begin a
serious conditioning program. Max
had read all the books. He had given
himself a stern talking-to in the mirror, and he
had gone to sleep listening to a positive motivational tape. Surely now he would be able to
overcome his klutziness!

"Okay, Max," PJ said. "Just keep thinking
positive!"

"I am!"

"Remember: You are as swift and graceful
as a gazelle!"

"I am!"

"Good!" PJ said with satisfaction. "Now . . .
get ready . . . get set . . .

GO!

Max was right, of course. The contests on Fitness Fun Day would be father-son affairs. PJ had the advantage. His father couldn't stand to lose, and would make sure both he and his son were in the proper condition and frame of mind to win.

What Max would have to do was even more difficult than changing his own attitude. He was going to have to turn his father into a non-klutz —not an easy task.

Max and PJ put their heads together. How could they change Goofy from clumsy to graceful? And in only a week? And without Goofy's finding out that they were trying to change him?

"I'm just gonna have to do for Dad what I did for myself," Max concluded.

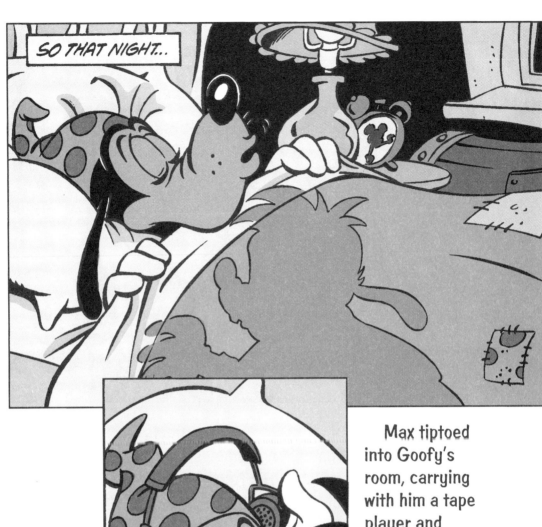

Max tiptoed into Goofy's room, carrying with him a tape player and headphones. On the player, he put a motivational tape—the same tape that had altered Max's own klutziness: "Overcoming the Absolutely IMPOSSIBLE!"

"There!" Max whispered, careful not to wake his dad. "Tomorrow he'll be a changed man."

Sure enough, the tape was working! Goofy didn't quite understand it, but he had the funny feeling that he could do just about anything!

Then, about to brush his teeth, he saw an odd sign taped to the bathroom mirror.

Because he didn't want his dad to realize that anything was different, Max invited Goofy to take a walk. Goofy saw no reason to refuse, so pretty soon he and Max were jogging down a path in the park. Little by little, Max picked up the pace, until they weren't just jogging, they were running!

"Hey, Max!" Goofy called. "Wait up! I thought we were goin' for a walk, not a run!"

"C'mon, Dad," Max called back, "running is better for you! It gets your blood pumping and everything. Just wait— you'll be a real athlete yet!"

Max leapt over a log that was lying across the path.

"Watch out, Dad!" he warned. "There's an obstacle ahead!"

WHOOOAA--!!

TRIP!

Max heard his father shout. He heard him stumble. He heard him fall in a heap. Uh-oh! he thought to himself. Maybe that tape isn't working as well as I thought.

Goofy began to pick himself up off the path. "Gawrsh!" he groaned. "I musta tripped."

And then some! Max thought. He turned back to help Goofy up.

"No," Max replied, "I just thought we should practice together, you know—father-son fitness, and all that?"

Goofy was touched. "Aw," he said, hugging his son, "you're the best kid a dad could want. You're always thinkin' of stuff for us to do together.

"This Saturday, we're gonna show everybody what a great team we are, by golly!"

Max gulped. He could just imagine what they would show everyone on Saturday . . .

"C'mon, Dad," Max sighed, with a weak smile. "Let's go home."

"Shore, son!" Goofy agreed, putting his arm around his son's shoulder. "I'll make us a nice, big breakfast. Nutrition is important, too, you know!"

That night, as Max slept, his thoughts turned again to Fitness Fun Day. His dream became a nightmare, with himself as the star!

Max awoke in a cold sweat. He would be a laughingstock! His father would be a laughingstock! And the one who would laugh the loudest would be Pete!

Max turned over and punched his pillow. Surely there was something he could do to avoid the humiliation that he was sure awaited himself and Goofy on Saturday!

Maybe he would break a leg. Nope—too painful.

Maybe it would snow on Saturday. Oh, right—in the middle of August!

Well, maybe the President would call him with a secret mission—yeah, and pigs fly!

Sore at heart, Max fell into an uneasy sleep.

Max's last hope was that at least there would be no picture in the paper of their futile tries to run.

AND SO, SATURDAY COMES AT LAST...

SHORE LOOKS LIKE *FUN*, HUH, MAX? LET'S FIND A SPOT TO *SET UP!*

I DON'T SEE ANY *PHOTOGRAPHERS!* MAYBE THEY'RE NOT *COMING!*

FITNESS FUN DAY

But even this hope was dashed when Goofy spotted a member of the local press. Max's heart sank. It was obvious that his dad had no idea how humiliating this day would prove.

THERE'S ONE, OVER AT THE *LONG JUMP PIT!*

SAY, THAT LOOKS LIKE *FUN!* LET'S *TRY* IT!

BUT--!

As Goofy stepped up to the line at the long-jump pit, Max crossed the fingers of both hands. Squeezing his eyes closed, he began to chant to himself, "Think positive! Think positive! He can do it!"

The crowd around the pit grew silent. Goofy shuffled his feet, trying to find the best stance for a good start.

Goofy swung his arms in big circles, like a windmill. He looked a little bit like a pitcher warming up—but the game wasn't baseball.

Then he jumped!

Of course, the dreaded photographer was there to take the dreaded photograph. It looked as if Max wasn't going to get any breaks!

He walked over to his dad, who was brushing sand off his legs and seat.

"Okay, Dad," he said with the best smile he could manage, "that was great! Why don't we take a break now?"

"A break?" Goofy repeated, startled. "Shucks, I'm just gettin' started. Let's go play some baseball," he suggested. "You like baseball, right?"

With a heavy heart, Max agreed that he did, indeed, like to play baseball. Before he knew it, his turn in the batting order came up. And of course the photographer decided that he'd taken enough pictures of the long jump and followed Max to the baseball diamond.

AND SO...

HERE IT *COMES*, MAX-- MUH FAMOUS *SPIN-CURVE-SLOW-FAST-TRIPLE-DECKER-WITH-WHIPPED-CREAM-ON-TOP BALL!*

BE POSITIVE, MAX... YOU'LL DO FINE...

WHACK!

YES!!

BOING!

As he lay on the ground beside home plate,
Max was disgusted. Boy, did that photographer
get a great picture! he thought to himself. I
can see it now, on the front page of the
Spoonerville Times: "Ball Beans Klutz"!
Sometimes I don't know why I bother!

Goofy rushed over. "Gawrsh, Max!" he said.
"Are you all right?"

"Sure, Dad,"
Max replied.

Later that day, Goofy and
Max joined Pete's family for lunch.

Pete turned to his wife, Peg. "Won't it?"

"Well, I don't know," Peg began. "What the
newspaper is really looking for is a picture of
somebody on the tilting tile floor."

"Gawrsh, what's that?" Goofy asked.

"It's a floor with tiles that tilt, so no one can
balance on it," answered PJ's sister, Pistol.

"But it's kinda dangerous," PJ warned.

With Pete's "help," Goofy convinced himself that the tilting tile floor was the competition for him. As soon as lunch was over, he dragged Max away.

"Come on, son," he urged, "this is gonna be lots of fun!"

Max wasn't so sure. So far they had bombed at the long jump, baseball, the relay race, the free-throw, and the hundred-yard dash. He didn't imagine they would do any better at this!

"Gee, Dad," he suggested, "maybe we should wait on this one."

Everyone is good at something, and Goofy was
no exception. The tilting tile floor seemed to
have been created just so that he could succeed.
    "Come on, Max!" he called. "You gotta try this!"
    And, as luck would have it, the tilting tile floor
seemed to have been created just so Max could
succeed, too!

As Goofy and Max danced gracefully all over the crazy surface, PJ ran to get his dad.

"Come look at Max and Goofy!" he cried. "The photographers are going crazy!"

Pete couldn't believe it. Why would those photographers want to take a picture of Goofy when they had all the photos they could want of him and PJ winning at arm wrestling?

"Don't just stand there," Peg scolded. "Let's try this thing!"

That's just what Peg, Pistol, Pete, PJ, and Goofy and Max did.

Saturday for Pete meant sports, sports, sports. From morning to night he would sit in his easy chair, hypnotized by the organized mayhem brought to him by the TV program, "Big Block of Sports."

Needless to say, his wife Peg didn't share this view. For her, Saturday was a day to get things done. And the one who should be getting things done, of course, was Pete.

Such a fundamental difference of opinion as to the purpose of Saturday was bound to cause conflict . . .

"Every Saturday it's the same thing!" huffed Peg. "I work like a dog, and you veg out in front of the TV set.

"Well, not **this** Saturday, Buster!"

Peg grabbed a newspaper, rolled it up, and smacked it smartly over her husband's head.

"Put up my posy fence, you big lummox!" she shouted.

WELCOME BACK TO SATURDAY'S BIG BLOCK OF SPORTS!

As soon as Peg was out of the room, Pete flopped back into his easy chair in front of the television set. What Peg didn't know wouldn't hurt her—or him, he figured.

As Pete's eyes glazed over, his daughter Pistol came skipping down the stairs, brandishing the Hypno-Blaster Instant Slave Gun that she had ordered from an ad in a comic book.

"Daddy, look!" she cried. "Wanna be my slave?"

"Never mind that," said her mother from the kitchen. "Daddy's going to build my posy fence, aren't you, dear?"

27

Once outside, Pete took refuge in the cabin
cruiser that he kept in his back yard.

"Heh, heh, heh!" he chuckled. "She'll never
think of looking for me here. I'll listen to the
ball game on the radio."

Meanwhile, Max arrived at PJ's just in time
to overhear Pistol talking about her new toy.

"See, Chainsaw?" she said to her dog. "I'm
going to use this on PJ, and make him my
slave for life."

The opportunity was too good for the boys to
pass up. They instantly decided they would
pretend to be enslaved.

"We'll show her no mercy!" snickered PJ.

The boys sidled into the living room. "Oh, hiya, sis," said PJ. Then both boys put on expressions of abject terror.

Pointing the Hypno-Blaster at her brother and his friend, Pistol pulled the trigger.

An eerie wail filled the air. Immediately Max and PJ went stiff as boards.

Pistol walked up to the boys. She waved her hand in front of their eyes. Both boys stared straight ahead, giving a very good imitation of being hypnotized.

Pistol turned to Chainsaw. "Golly!" she breathed.

IT *WORKED!* IT *WORKED!* YOU'RE *BOTH* MY *SLAVES!*

WE ARE YOUR SLAVES.

"Oh, wow! My slaves!" She thought for a minute. "Now, what will I make you do?" she wondered out loud.

Pistol was so excited she didn't see the wink that passed between Max and her brother.

Out in the back yard, Pete was watching his neighbor from the comfort of his cruiser.

"Look at that Goof down there, wastin' a beautiful Saturday mornin' doin' yard work!" Pete sniggered. "An' he don't even have a wife to badger him into it!"

"What an idiot!"

Goofy had no idea that he was being watched. He was happy mowing his lawn.

Mowing the lawn on Saturday mornings was one of his greatest pleasures. There was something, well, therapeutic about it.

Goofy wasn't paying any attention to the yard next door, where Pistol had marched the boys outside to give them their orders.

PJ and Max marched around the yard, flapping their arms like wings and acting for all the world like chickens scratching for food.

Pistol was impressed. Her Hypno-Blaster was really something!

What none of the children knew was how far the Hypno-Blaster's mesmerizing tone would reach. Its power beamed all the way across the back fence and into the next yard.

When Pistol pulled the trigger, her gun's hypnotic squeal found an unexpected target!

"Okay, now you're doggies!" Pistol commanded.

As P.J and Max started hopping around the yard and barking, Pete watched Goofy get down on all fours and pick up a rake in his teeth.

Just then, PJ and Max couldn't keep their faces straight any longer. They let Pistol in on the joke.

"You mean you're **not** my slaves?" she wailed.

"Sorry, Pistol," said PJ. "No hard feelin's, okay? C'mon, let's get some ice cream."

As the kids went back in the house, Pete climbed down and picked up Pistol's pistol.

"I'll be switched!" he said. "The kid was onto some- thing!"

"Hypnotizin' gun, eh?" he said to himself, glancing over the fence at Goofy, who was prancing around on all fours, barking and growling.

He aimed the gun at Goofy and pulled the trigger.

"Okay, you're normal!" Pete ordered.

Goofy came to himself and stood up. "Say, Pete, that's a keen toy gun," he said. "What does it do?"

Pete pointed it at Goofy. "Allow me to demonstrate," he began.

Suddenly Peg's voice floated over to them. "Pete!" she called. "I know you're hiding out there somewhere!"

THE KIDS AND I ARE GOING *SHOPPING!* HAVE THE YARD WORK *FINISHED* BY THE TIME I GET *BACK,* SNOOKUMS--

-- OR ELSE!!

HEH HEH! I'LL DO BETTER'N *THAT!*

I'LL GET THIS *DOOFUS* TO DO IT *FOR ME!*

GOOFY, YOU'RE MY SLAVE!

I AM YER SLAVE.

WHEEE

OKAY, NOW *LISTEN--* SEE THAT PILE OF WHITE *PICKETS* OVER HERE? I *ORDER* YOU TO PUT UP A *FENCE* AROUND PEG'S *POSIES* WHILE I WATCH *TV! GOT* THAT?

HYUK! GOT IT.

"Pete, you devil!" he congratulated himself as he strolled in the house and sat back down in his easy chair. "You're too clever for your own good. Goofy does all your work, an' Peg'll never know.

"An' neither will the Goof! Har, har, har!"

As Pete sat down to concentrate once more on the "Big Block of Sports," the sounds of hammering and pounding floated in from the back yard.

Then came Goofy's voice. "All done, Master!" he announced.

"What?" Pete was astounded. No one could work that fast, hypnotized or not.

Pete picked up the Hypno-Blaster and stomped out to the back yard. He groaned when he saw what Goofy had done.

Pete slammed back into the house. "Stupid, bone-headed, blubber-brained, flipper-footed dope!" he groused. "He better get it right this time!"

"All done, Master!" Goofy called.

"Wait a minute!" Pete said, puzzled. Again he marched out to the back yard. And again he found something that made him mad.

"Now, listen real good!" he yelled at his slave. "Build a fence around the posy garden—just the posy garden, got that? Something that'll keep the dog out! Think you can handle that?"

"Shore, Master," said Goofy, saluting.

Back in front of "Big Block of Sports," Pete grabbed a big bowl of popcorn. "I wonder if bein' hypnotized makes a stupid guy stupider," he mused.

"All done, Master!" the call came again.

Pete grabbed Goofy by the collar. "Listen, you numbskull!" he growled. "I've had enough out of you! Get rid of this bomb shelter and build a cute little fence. A kinda dainty, frilly fence, 'cause that's what Peg wants, see?!"

"Okey-dokey," Goofy mumbled.

Pete dragged himself back inside. "I gotta watch some sports," he mumbled. "It's a known fact that sports is relaxin'."

Pete waited to hear sounds of fence-building. Nothing. Then . . .

I'LL KILL YOU!!

NO, *WAIT!* I *CAN'T* KILL YOU! NO *TIME!* GOTTA GET THAT *POSY GARDEN* BACK IN SHAPE BEFORE *PEG* COMES HOME!

Pete ran back into the house. "Gotta buy more flowers!" he panted. "Gotta replant 'em! Gotta hurry! Oh, do I **hate** yard work!"

As Pete hustled away, his last words gradually got through to Goofy. Still under the spell of the Hypno-Blaster, Goofy pulled himself together. If Pete said "yard work," then yard work was what Goofy would do.

"Yard work!" he intoned. "Must do yard work!"

Well, what else does a man use to do yard work? A lawn mower, of course. And since it was Pete's lawn, Goofy had to use Pete's lawn mower, a 98-horsepower, 15-speed, **fine** mowing machine.

Pete came home to a terrifying sight.

YEAAGH!!

STOP, YOU MORON! STO-O-O-OP!

WHERE'S THAT CRAMFRATTIN' *HYPNOTIZIN'* GUN?!

It finally became clear to Pete that his plot to make Goofy do all his—Pete's—yard work was going to backfire. Peg was due home any minute.

And Peg would not be pleased.

Frantically, Pete looked around for Pistol's toy gun. Maybe he had left it in the house. He dashed inside.

The gun wasn't by his easy chair, or in the pop-corn bowl, or in the kitchen. What on earth could he do?

Pete ran back outside.

40

But Goofy would not be stopped. Yard work
Pete had commanded, and yard work his slave
would do. The pool was in the way. The pool
would be mowed down.

Helpless, Pete watched Goofy crash his fine
mowing machine straight into the pool.

Pete cringed.

Goofy floored it.

"Please let him turn!" Pete begged. He shut his eyes, unable to watch.

The mower motor revved. Pete heard its wheels go from grass to concrete.

Then came the sound he dreaded.

Of course, Peg picked this precise moment to come home. The sight that met her eyes would have made a stronger woman weep.

Peg gasped.

So did Pistol, so did PJ, and so did Max, who all crowded in the door behind her.

Pete knew he was in for it. He waved weakly.

43

There was nothing Pete could say that would cool Peg down. As she stalked into the living room, he looked around frantically for someone else to blame. His eyes fell on Goofy, who was sitting on the 98-horsepower, 15-speed, fine mowing machine, watching "Big Block of Sports."

"It was his fault!" he whined. "Look! There he is, caught in the act! I didn't have anything to do with it! Honest!"

Peg wasn't fooled. She knew a culprit when she saw one. She grabbed her husband by the collar.

"You mean my Hypno-Blaster really works?" cried Pistol. "Wow! Lemme try!"

She spied the slave gun, grabbed it, pointed it at Goofy, and pulled the trigger.

Pistol whispered something to her mother.

"Why, Pistol, darling, what a wonderful idea!" said Peg. "Let me try."

Peg pointed the gun at Pete and pulled the trigger.

It was a kind of poetic justice. Pete fell victim to the Hypno-Blaster, just as Goofy had.

"Pete, darling," Peg cooed. "I have something for you to do."

Like a robot—or like the slave he had become—Pete marched out to the back yard to begin the hated yard work.

As night fell in Spoonerville, Goofy got ready for some well-earned rest. But next door, poor Pete was still hard at work . . .

46